Mystery Pups

DIAMOND DOGS!

Mystery Pups

DIAMOND DOGS!

by Jodie Mellor

Illustrated by Penny Dann

SIMON AND SCHUSTER

SIMON AND SCHUSTER
First published in Great Britain in 2009 by Simon and Schuster UK Ltd
A CBS COMPANY

Simon & Schuster UK Ltd
1st Floor, 222 Gray's Inn Road, London WC1X 8HB.

This book is a work of fiction. Names, characters, places and incidents are either the
product of the author's imagination or are used fictitiously. Any resemblance to actual
people living or dead, events or locales is entirely coincidental.

A CIP catalogue record for this book is available from the British Library.

ISBN: 978-1-84738-227-6

Printed and bound in Great Britain
by CPI Cox and Wyman, Reading, Berkshire RG1 8EX

www.simonandschuster.co.uk

Chapter One

'Hush!' Caitlin warned her friends, Megan and Lauren.

The three girls sat on the grass in Megan's garden, ready to make their Magic Mountain Puppy Club promises. Their puppies, Dylan and Buster, yipped and wagged their tails. Caitlin's toy dog, Daisy, didn't blink.

'Why are we hushing? What's wrong?' Lauren asked.

'I thought I heard someone open the gate!' Caitlin hissed. The girls had sworn not to let anyone in on the secret of their magical mystery pups.

'It's the postman!' Megan said, peering over a low hedge. 'It's OK, he's leaving.'

'So now can we make our promises and give the pups their medallions?' Lauren demanded. As always, she was eager to get on.

Megan and Caitlin nodded. 'Are you ready, Dylan?' Megan asked her bright-eyed black Labrador pup.

Dylan yapped then raised himself onto his haunches. His front paws dangled as he waited for Megan to hang his medallion around his neck.

'Ready, Buster?' Lauren asked her bouncy, scruffy-haired pup.

'Yip!' Buster could hardly wait for his red ribbon and gold medal.

'Ready?' Caitlin said softly to cuddly-toy Daisy.

The light twinkled in Daisy's shiny dark eyes but she didn't move.

'We are members of the Magic Mountain Puppy Club,' the girls chanted solemnly. 'We

promise to feed and play with our puppies...'

The sun shone down on Megan's garden in her quiet street. Next door, someone was mowing the lawn.

'. . . and we promise to take our puppies for long walks.' Megan, Caitlin and Lauren finished their promises then leaned forward to hang the gold medallions around their necks.

'There!' Megan sighed happily. The sunlight glinted on Dylan's gold medallion.

'We did it!' Caitlin stared at Daisy, waiting for the magic to start.

'But it's not happening!' Lauren frowned. Where was the bright light that would whoosh them off on an adventure? Why weren't they floating and whirling through space to Sleuth City?

'Maybe it doesn't happen every time,' Megan said quietly. 'Or only when there's a crime that needs solving.' She gazed up at the blue sky.

'Please, please come alive,' Caitlin whispered to Daisy, picking her up and giving her a hug.

Daisy put out her little pink tongue and licked Caitlin's hand. 'Yes!' Caitlin said quietly, her green eyes shining.

The drone of the lawn mower grew faint, the world seemed to tilt and spin...

'Here we go!' Lauren cried. She floated free of the ground then twisted and tumbled like a spaceman in outer space.

'Magic!' Megan breathed as a brilliant white light surrounded them.

The three pups bounded ahead through mid-air. The light grew until it dazzled. Caitlin, Megan and Lauren shut their eyes, and *whoosh*!

When they opened them again they were slap bang in the magical world of Sleuth City.

CHAPTER TWO

'Spooky!' Lauren whispered.

It was the middle of the night and the city was cloaked in darkness. Tall buildings rose up on all sides.

'The whole city is asleep,' Megan murmured. She peered through a big shop window at dummies dressed in the latest fashions. Down the street, Dylan, Buster and Daisy sniffed at rubbish bags piled up by the kerb.

A yellow cab crawled by, stopped at a red light, then drove on.

'The streets feel weird when they're empty,' Caitlin said. 'I like it better when it's daylight and there are loads of people around.'

Just then, the pups came running over to the girls. They barked, then ran off again down the street.

'They want us to follow,' Megan guessed.

The girls sprinted after the pups, past a book shop and a bank. Dylan sniffed at the sidewalk, ahead of Buster and Daisy, who followed him, yapping loudly.

'I wonder what they've spotted.' Caitlin stared up and down the empty street at the glowing shop lights and the winking traffic signals.

'I don't know, but we always come here for a reason,' Megan insisted. 'Remember, they're our super-sleuth, magic pups!'

'Mega-spooky!' Lauren breathed. In a shop doorway, the wind rustled through pages of an old newspaper, lifted them in the air and swirled them against the girls' legs.

Dylan, Daisy and Buster trotted eagerly

forward. They looked tiny on the wide sidewalks, with the buildings towering overhead.

Waah-waah! A distant police siren grew louder then faded away.

'Uh-oh – the puppies seem interested in that van.' Megan pointed to a solitary white vehicle parked outside a shop. The shop had a metal security grille across the window and doorway.

'Take a look at this diamond necklace!' Caitlin exclaimed, pressing her nose against the grille. There was a display of expensive jewellery in the window. 'And another one with rubies. And, wow, look at that massive, sparkly ring!'

As Megan went to stare at the jewels, Lauren joined the puppies by the van. 'What is it? What's wrong?' she muttered.

Buster yapped and jumped up at the back door, which silently swung open.

'Huh!' Lauren peered inside. The van was

empty except for a couple of big cardboard boxes. 'Fancy leaving the door unlocked!'

'Did you ever see such a huge diamond!' Caitlin pointed out another ring in the jeweller's window. She and Megan were totally thrilled by what they saw.

'Mega-bling!' Megan sighed. It was the kind of stuff worn by movie stars.

Meanwhile, lively Buster jumped up again, took a sniff inside the van, then hopped inside.

'Come back, Buster!' Lauren hissed, watching his furry rear end disappear into the van.

'Yip!' Daisy called. Her legs were too short to follow.

'Yap!' Sensible Dylan ran to attract Megan's attention.

'Come out of there!' Lauren demanded. She could hear Buster's paws scrabbling against the metal floor of the van. 'Buster, do as you're told!'

It was no good – she would have to climb in there and fetch him.

Lauren had one foot on the back bumper and was just heaving herself into the van when the shop alarm burst into life.

At the window, Caitlin and Megan jumped back as if they'd been stung. For a split second they thought they'd set off the burglar alarm themselves. But then there was the sound of glass shattering in a first floor window and the sight of a man dressed in black climbing out.

The man perched on the window ledge, spotted Megan and Caitlin, plus Dylan and Daisy, then turned to warn his accomplice. 'We've been spotted by a couple of kids!' he yelled, taking a heavy bag from the man inside before turning to slide down the canvas awning, then leap to the ground.

'Watch out!' Caitlin pressed Megan back against the shop window. The thief had narrowly missed them as he jumped with the bag. She caught a glimpse of his face under the shadowy peak of a baseball cap – narrowed, glinting grey eyes, a long nose and thin mouth. His chin was covered in grey stubble.

'Oof!' Megan's shoulders thudded against the grille.

Then the second man slid down the awning

16

and jumped awkwardly to the ground. He limped heavily after the first thief, towards the parked van. 'Joey, throw the bag in the back!' he yelled. 'I've hurt my leg. You'll have to drive!'

The first thief flung the heavy hold-all into the back of the van where Lauren cowered with Buster. She heard the key turn in the lock. Then the man ran to the front, leaped into the driver's seat and waited for the limping accomplice to join him. 'Get a move on, Eddie!' he snarled, above the shrill wail of the shop alarm. 'The cops will be here any second!'

'No – wait!' Megan cried out in panic as she saw Lauren being locked in. She rushed towards the back door of the van and started to wrench at the handle.

The driver started the engine and put his foot on the accelerator. Dylan, Daisy and Caitlin ran in front of the van.

'Stop!' Caitlin pleaded, waving her arms wildly.

But the driver screeched away from the kerb and Caitlin and the puppies had to leap out of his path. At the back of the van, Megan let go of the handle. She sat down heavily on the road, watching the red tail lights disappear.

Inside the dark van, Lauren and Buster were thrown this way and that. The driver took corners on two wheels, brakes screeching, tyres squealing. Lauren crashed against the van wall and toppled on to the floor. Buster whined as he slid into the bag containing the thieves' haul.

'Buster, are you OK?' At last Lauren found a ledge to hold on to. Her knuckles turned white and her stomach churned.

The puppy whimpered as the hold-all slid across the floor and slammed into the side, spilling its glittering contents - stolen watches, bracelets and rings, diamond necklaces and brooches - haphazardly across the floor.

'Oh!' Lauren gasped. 'Buster, look at that!'

The van screeched round another corner and Lauren lost her grip, tumbling against an empty box, her hair in her face, her elbows and knees scratched by the raw metal.

And the priceless jewels slid around the floor of the van, while back at the jeweller's shop, the burglar alarm rang out and police cars raced to the scene.

CHAPTER THREE

'OK, it's pretty obvious what happened here.' The first policeman to step out of his car looked up at the broken first-floor window and the bent awning of the burgled jewellery shop. 'We're not certain how the thieves got in, but we sure know which way they got out!'

'There were two of them,' Megan gabbled. 'They were dressed in black, wearing baseball caps. They were in a white van.'

'And they drove away with our friend!' Caitlin said. She felt shaky all over and tried hard not to cry.

'Hold on,' the cop told her. 'You didn't touch

anything, did you?'

'Yip! Yap!' Dylan and Daisy ran in the direction the thieves' van had taken.

'We haven't touched a thing!' Megan insisted. 'We tried to stop them from driving off with Lauren and Buster, but they just ignored us and sped away.'

'We're really worried about Lauren,' Caitlin gasped. 'She's in the back of the van with a bag of stolen jewels. What'll happen when the thieves find her?'

'And Buster,' Megan added.

'Stand there,' the cop ordered, before asking for the area to be taped off and for more support from fellow officers. 'Send a crime scene team to Royale Jewellers on Fourth Street,' he said into his two-way radio. 'There's been a break-in. We're holding on to some witnesses – a couple of kids. Don't worry – I'll bring them in for questioning as soon as we're finished here.'

'No, don't do that!' Caitlin gasped. 'We have to find Lauren and Buster first!'

'Stay!' the cop said, wagging his finger as if he was giving orders to two disobedient dogs.

'You don't move from this spot until we've taken a look inside the shop, OK?'

'What do we do now?' Lauren asked Buster.

As the van screeched and screamed down the empty city streets, she tried to gather up the spilt jewellery. But the rings rolled into crevices and the necklaces slid and snaked under cardboard boxes.

Buster yapped, then tugged at Lauren's T-shirt. He tried to drag her towards the nearest box.

'You want me to hide in there?' she guessed. She decided to crawl across the floor and investigate, lifting up the flaps and discovering that the box was empty. 'Good idea!' she agreed.

And it wasn't a moment too soon – suddenly Joey the driver slammed on the brakes and the van screeched to a halt.

'Quick!' Lauren hissed at Buster. 'We can both fit inside here!'

As they hid in the box, the thieves came to

the back door and climbed inside.

'All the stuff's fallen out of the bag!' Eddie groaned at what he saw.

'Grab it!' Joey ordered. 'Shove it back in, quick!'

Inside the box, Lauren put her finger to her lips to tell Buster to be quiet. She hardly dared breathe.

'None of this was meant to happen,' Joey grumbled. 'Dino was supposed to leave that upstairs window open for our escape.'

'Yeah, well, you've done this often enough to know things don't always go to plan,' Eddie grunted. 'We smashed the window and got away, didn't we?'

'But what about those two kids?' Joey had taken off his leather gloves and was on his hands and knees, picking up the scattered jewels. 'One of them got a good look at me.'

'Forget it. They were just a couple of street kids.'

Lauren felt one of the thieves tip the box she was in and search underneath it. She held on to Buster and swallowed hard. *This is it!* she thought. *He's going to look inside!*

'OK – enough'. Eddie was through searching. He closed the zipper on the bag. 'If we've left anything behind, Russ will pick it up when he clears the van and takes it back to the car hire place.'

'Yeah, and you think he'll come clean and tell us if he finds a ring worth a cool half a million?' Joey scoffed.

Just go! Lauren prayed.

'Joey, leave it!' Eddie had begun to walk away, but now he came back. 'We've got to get out of here.'

Joey pushed hard at the box where Lauren was hiding. Easing it into the corner, he discovered a bright diamond ring on the dirty floor. 'Got it!' he cried.

'OK, happy now?' Eddie held the door open

and Joey jumped out, holding up the
ring in triumph.

'How bad is your leg? Can you walk?' Joey
asked.

'I'll make it to Mickey's', Eddie assured him.

But Lauren heard him groan as he put his
weight on the injured leg. She only began to
breathe again as she heard their voices fading
into the distance.

'OK, Buster!' she whispered when the
footsteps had ceased. Carefully she lifted the
box flaps and peered out. Then she and her
pup climbed out.

Buster ran straight to the other
box and nudged it with his nose.
He seized a shiny necklace hidden
beneath.

'Good boy!' Lauren whispered,
picking the necklace up and
slipping it in her jeans pocket. Then
she ventured towards the door.

'Wow, it's dark out here!' she whispered. 'And I haven't a clue where we are!'

'OK, so you say there were two thieves?' The stern police sergeant had left his men searching the premises of Royale Jewellers and come back on to the street to question Megan and Caitlin.

Megan nodded. 'One was tall. I didn't get a good look at him, but I think he hurt his leg when he jumped. The other one was shorter. His face was kind of thin and mean. He needed a shave.'

'We have to go!' Caitlin protested. Every second they wasted here, the harder it would be for Dylan and Daisy to track down the white van.

But the sergeant kept them inside the taped-off area, beside the flashing orange lights of two police cars.

'Did you get the registration number of the

vehicle?' the sergeant asked, folding his arms, not expecting a yes.

Quickly Megan reeled off the number.

'Smart kid, huh?' the burly sergeant grunted. He made a note of the information then called his precinct office. 'Trace this van for me, would you?'

'Now can we go?' Caitlin begged.

'How come you were out here on the streets at this time of night?' the sergeant said, ignoring Caitlin and concentrating on Megan.

'We were walking our puppies!' Megan answered a shade too quickly.

A few paces away, Dylan and Daisy tried hard to look like dogs who were being taken for a quiet walk.

The sergeant didn't like Megan's slick answer. He raised an eyebrow. 'So where do you live?' he asked suspiciously.

This time Megan took her time. 'Erm – we're just visiting Sleuth City. We don't actually live here.'

'No address?' The cop tutted. Then his radio came on and he turned away from Megan and Caitlin to listen to new details about the white van.
'It's an out-of-town number – yeah, I got that. Registered to White Arrow car hire company…'

As he talked, Caitlin grabbed Megan's hand. 'Let's get out of here!' she whispered. 'Now!'

Megan nodded. The two girls made a run for it, ducking under the police cordon and following Daisy and Dylan across the well-lit street, darting down a dark alleyway and out of sight.

'OK, Buster, what next?' Lauren felt scared as she stepped gingerly from the white van on to the rough, gravel-covered ground.

The thieves, Eddie and Joey, had disappeared into the night and she found she was in an unlit area in the shadow of a tall office block and overlooking a stretch of steely grey water.

'That must be the river,' she decided, spotting a row of white lights winking on the distant shore. 'And this looks like a big construction site.'

Buster ran here and there, sniffing at wire fencing, steel girders and stacks of concrete blocks. Then he trotted towards an open gateway.

'Wait for me!' Lauren called after him, shivering in the cold wind from the river. This place was bleak and lonely. She set off after Buster, away from the van ... and into a weak, wobbly shaft of yellow light!

'Woof!' Buster stopped dead in the pool of light cast by the torch beam. His dark eyes gleamed.

'Who's there?' Lauren asked shakily.

The torch beam flashed from Buster to her then back again.

Maybe Eddie and Joey have changed their minds and come back to search the van! Lauren thought.

'Who is it?' she asked nervously.

Footsteps crunched over the gravel surface. The torch beam wobbled back towards Lauren.

'Security,' a gruff man's voice answered. 'It's my job to patrol this area.'

'Thank goodness!' Lauren stood in the weak spotlight and heaved a sigh of relief. As the man walked towards her, she could make out silver buttons gleaming on his uniform.

'You're trespassing,' he told Lauren sternly.

'I can explain,' she stammered. The light was growing stronger, dazzling her so that she couldn't see the man's face.

'OK, go ahead,' he invited. 'Tell me – what's a decent kid like you doing on a construction site in the middle of the night?'

CHAPTER FOUR

'Don't look back!' Caitlin warned Megan.

They were following Dylan and Daisy down a side street, sprinting as fast as they could.

Megan ignored Caitlin and glanced over her shoulder. 'Let me see if the police are coming after us,' she gasped.

Sure enough, there was the sound of footsteps running across the main street.

'This way!' Caitlin cried, diving down an alleyway after the two pups. Dylan raced along, swerving around a parked motorbike and splashing through a dark puddle. Dainty Daisy avoided the puddle and yapped for

Caitlin and Megan to hurry.

Desperately, the girls darted down the seedy alley, praying that the cops would take a wrong turn.

'I'm scared for Lauren!' Caitlin admitted. Her heart thumped as she squeezed past a tall wheelie bin overflowing with rubbish.

'Me too,' Megan admitted. 'But we just have

to follow Dylan and Daisy. I know they'll find her for us.'

The pups took another turning, then another. Soon they'd left the cops in a side street, wondering which way to go.

'Slow down!' Caitlin pleaded, once she was sure they weren't being followed. 'I need to catch my breath.'

Megan nodded. 'What a mess we're in!' she sighed, bending to stroke Dylan, who came up eagerly. 'Yes, I know you want us to follow. But we're not as fast as you.'

The little Labrador wagged his tail. His ears were pricked, as if he was picking up sounds from far away.  Then he barked and tugged at Megan's sleeve.

'What? I can't hear anything!' she muttered. Only an eerie city hum –

perhaps cars in the distance.

'OK, we're ready!' she said, taking a deep breath.

So Dylan and Daisy charged on again, listening hard and taking a dozen different dark turnings until they came out onto a wide dual carriageway.

'You want us to cross *this*?' Caitlin asked, looking left and right at the cars cruising by.

The pups yapped then seized their chance to sprint across the road.

They dodged the traffic and darted under a steel barrier, down a dark slope.

Caitlin glanced at Megan, who shrugged. 'Don't do this at home!' she joked weakly.

'Here goes!' Caitlin waited for a safe gap between the cars, nodded at Megan and together they dashed after Daisy and Dylan.

'I can explain everything!' Lauren told the security guard eagerly. She was flooded with relief after the wild ride in the back of the getaway van. 'I was walking down Fourth Street with my friends, Megan and Caitlin. We were minding our own business ...'

The guard aimed the torch straight at Lauren's face. 'Cut to the chase,' he ordered.

'How come you and your dog are snooping around here?'

'You see that white van?' Lauren gabbled. 'I arrived in the back of it. It was used in a big jewel robbery on Fourth Street. The thieves dumped it here!'

'You don't say!' the man grunted.

Lauren frowned. She wished she could see his face, but the torch beam still dazzled her. 'I'm serious. And if you don't believe me, take a look at this!' She slid her hand in her pocket and drew out the diamond necklace.

'Let me see that!' The guard snatched the necklace from her. The gems sparkled in the torchlight and his hand shook. 'You'd better come with me to the office and tell me exactly how you got hold of this.'

'I don't like this one little bit!' Caitlin muttered. Empty city streets were bad enough, but the dark, gloomy slope at the far side of the highway was worse. She tripped over a burst tyre and slid on her backside to join Daisy and Dylan at the bottom.

Megan soon caught them up. 'We're on the edge of town, close to the river,' she guessed. 'It's definitely the sort of lonely place thieves would choose to dump a getaway car.'

'With Lauren and Buster inside,' Caitlin reminded her with a shudder.

'I'm trying not to think about that. Look – Daisy and Dylan are ready to move on.'

Fresh and eager as ever, the pups led the way, sniffing for a scent, then raising their heads to listen, until they came to a wire fence.

'Oh, no, a dead end!' Megan groaned.

'But you were right about the river,' Caitlin muttered, pointing to the gleam of murky water and listening to the lap of waves against a concrete pier.

'And Dylan and Daisy were right about everything else!' Megan's sharp eyes had spotted a white van beyond the fence – the white van that the thieves had used to escape!

'Good dogs!' Caitlin breathed, as Daisy and Dylan ran off towards the river. She hooked her fingers through the wire netting and stared straight ahead at the getaway van. 'Please let Lauren and Buster be safe!' she begged. 'Please don't let anything horrible happen to them!'

'Buster, be good!' Lauren was puzzled. Why was he yapping at the security guard?

'Follow me,' the guard said, holding on to the diamond necklace and leading Lauren to a small cabin beside the entrance to the construction site. He opened the door and turned on the light. 'Sit down,' he said, pointing to a swivel chair behind a cluttered desk.

Still unhappy, Buster crept under the desk and kept up a low growl.

'You have to call the police!' Lauren insisted. 'There were two robbers. They smashed a jewellery shop window and jumped out.'

The security guard took off his cap and put it on the desk. He was frowning as he stared at the spectacular diamond necklace.

'Why don't you believe me?' Lauren cried. 'Surely that necklace is proof that I'm telling the truth?'

'Shut up for a second and let me think.'

Under the fluorescent light, the guard looked pale and tired. He was a big man of about fifty, with a bald head and a grey goatee beard.

'Call the police!' Lauren pleaded.

At last the guard nodded and picked up the phone. Lauren heaved a sigh. 'It's OK, Buster – we'll soon be out of here!'

Under the desk, the mongrel pup rested his chin on his front paws, watching every move the guard made.

'Hey, it's me – Russ', he said into the phone. He let the diamond necklace dangle from his stubby fingers. 'Something unexpected has happened at the construction site.'

He must be calling his boss before he contacts the police, Lauren thought. *I wish he'd get a move on!*

Buster growled again.

'Yeah, the White Arrow van's

44

still here, the guard said into the phone.

Suddenly the hairs at the back of Lauren's neck began to prickle. Who was he talking to, and why was he calmly talking about the getaway van?

Russ listened for a while then spoke again. 'Hold on – you didn't know it, but a kid and a puppy were in the back of the van – yeah.'

And then a memory flashed in Lauren's brain of Joey talking to Eddie. "If we've left anything behind, Russ will pick it up when he clears the van …"

Russ! The name of their accomplice. *And* the name of this security guard.

Lauren jumped up from the chair and made a dash for the cabin door. Russ got there before her and barred her way. 'Joey, I've got to go,' he said into the phone. 'I'll find you at Mickey's place – OK?'

'Let me go!' Lauren yelled at the traitor in the security guard's uniform. She kicked his shins while Buster bit his ankles.

But Russ shook Buster off and grabbed Lauren by both arms. He lifted her off her feet and dumped her on the swivel chair, taking off his tie to bind her hands behind her back then tie her to the chair. Lauren kicked and struggled, but she knew she was too weak to win.

Once Lauren's hands were tied, he turned and grabbed the puppy by the scruff of the neck.

'Get the heck out of here!' Russ snarled. Then he opened the door and tossed Buster outside.

CHAPTER FIVE

Lauren heard Buster yelp and caught a glimpse of the white van before the cabin door slammed shut.

'Stupid, interfering kid!' Russ sneered. He leaned forward to dangle the diamond necklace close to her face. Then he smiled and shoved it into his jacket pocket. 'Yeah, I know!' he scoffed. 'You're sorry you ever got involved in this!'

'Here comes Buster!' It was Caitlin who spotted him first. She was still standing at the wire fence, staring into the deserted construction site.

Megan had followed Dylan and Daisy down to the water's edge, only to discover that there was no way round the fence. She was gazing down into the deep, dark water when Caitlin cried out.

Dusty and dishevelled, Lauren's pup was bounding across the construction site towards Caitlin.

'Where did *you* appear from?' she asked, trying to prise up the bottom of the wire netting so Buster could squeeze underneath.

He yapped, then ran back towards the security guard's cabin by the gate.

'This way!' Caitlin called softly to Megan, Dylan and Daisy. 'There's a light on over here!'

'Sshhh!' Megan warned. 'This feels all wrong. Where's Lauren?'

Buster answered her question by running to scratch at the cabin door.

Megan and Caitlin stayed out of sight as the door opened and a man's voice yelled angrily at Buster. 'Get out of here – beat it!' He aimed a kick and missed.

'Ouch!' Caitlin cringed as Buster dodged the man's boot. 'That was vicious!'

The slam of the door made them shiver.

Inside the cabin, Russ turned back to Lauren. 'OK, don't even *think* about yelling for help', he told her.

Lauren bit her lip and nodded.

'I need some answers. First – what happened to your friends – the ones Joey says you were with outside the jewellers?'

'I don't know. They stayed behind when Buster and I got into the van.'

'So the cops will know about the van.' Russ paced up and down then glanced out of the cabin window. The getaway van stood there large as life. 'Too risky to drive it back to the White Arrow depot,' he decided.

Lauren watched Russ pace some more, then come to a decision. Pulling open a desk drawer, he reached inside and took out a box of matches. Then he seized a plastic can from the corner of the room.

'No!' Lauren panicked. She smelt petrol as Russ unscrewed the top.

'You have the best seat in the house,' he told her. 'This baby is going to light up the sky!' Then he took the can and ran out of the cabin towards the van.

'What's that weird smell?' Megan whispered as the cabin door opened and a man emerged. She held on tight to Dylan and kept out of sight.

'It smells like petrol!' Caitlin muttered. Daisy quivered at her side.

But Buster wasn't afraid. He ran straight at the man's ankles, growling and snapping, as the guard flung the contents of the can over the van.

Soon Dylan and Daisy joined in. They escaped from Megan and Caitlin and charged the enemy, locking on to his leg and tearing at his trousers.

Still Russ didn't stop. Though the pups were fighting him for all they were worth, he dipped an old rag into the can, struck a match, lit the petrol-soaked rag and threw it at the van.

There was a giant whoosh and a blinding flash as the petrol ignited.

'Dylan, Daisy, come here!' Megan and Caitlin cried out for their pups. Orange flames shot into the air. All they could see was the dark silhouette of a man staggering back from the fierce fire.

Through the window, Lauren saw Dylan and Daisy join Buster. It meant that Megan and Caitlin couldn't be far away. 'Help!' she cried. 'I'm in here!'

As Russ staggered and fell to the ground, the puppies kept up their attack. Caitlin and Megan came out of hiding and sprinted to the cabin, bursting through the door.

'Untie me!' Lauren pleaded

But the knot was too tight. 'I can't undo it!' Megan gasped.

So Caitlin searched the desk drawer and found a pair of scissors. She used them to snip through the tie.

Outside, flames leapt into the air. In the

distance, sirens sounded as a fire team raced through the streets. Russ was still down, crawling away from the heat of the fire, unable to shake off the pups.

'Are you OK?' Caitlin asked Lauren.

Lauren was trembling but she nodded. 'It was a nightmare,' she confessed. 'I've never been so scared.'

'Me neither,' Caitlin admitted. And it still wasn't over. There was a fire raging outside and the three puppies were struggling with a desperate man.

'His name's Russ. He's part of the gang,' Lauren told them. 'We mustn't let him get away!'

So, as the fire engine drew near, the girls ran to help Dylan, Buster and Daisy.

'Call them off!' Russ pleaded as the girls approached. The fire cast a flickering red light over his scared, exhausted face.

Just then there was a loud explosion and a

shower of sparks rose from the burning van.

For a moment, the startled puppies lost hold of Russ – just long enough for him to scramble to his feet and run off. He sprinted blindly away from the flames, towards the river.

Sparks drifted down around the girls' heads. They stood in shock.

Meanwhile, Russ reached the concrete pier. He stared down at the oily black water. Then, stopping only to kick off his boots, he dived in.

CHAPTER SIX

The girls held their breaths.

They waited for Russ to re-surface.

Ripples spread across the water, but there was no sign of him.

The puppies too peered over the edge of the pier and waited.

Behind them, the fire team drove into the construction lot, lights flashing, siren wailing. Half a dozen men jumped down from the vehicle, carrying cans of chemical spray. They aimed the nozzles at the burning van.

But the driver of the fire engine had stayed in his cab and was taking in the surrounding scene. Suddenly he spotted the three girls. He climbed down from the cab. 'Hey!' he shouted. 'I need to talk to you!'

Caitlin, Megan and Lauren whirled round. Their heads were already spinning, their stomachs churning. They felt sure that Russ had drowned.

'Did you kids start this fire?' The driver strode towards them, his yellow helmet reflecting the flickering light of the flames.

'We could be in serious trouble!' Lauren groaned. She felt Buster hang back for once.

'What do we do?' Caitlin muttered.

Lauren thought fast. She knew the fire officer would ask them loads of difficult questions and this would slow them down. 'We run!' she decided.

The fire officer was only a few paces away, his face grim and suspicious.

'OK', Megan agreed. 'But this time we stick together. We don't split up, whatever happens!'

They fled past the fire officer, across the construction site. They jumped over girders and concrete blocks, darted past the cabin and out of the gate.

'Keep up, Daisy!' Caitlin willed the little Yorkie to escape the angry firefighter's clutches. The moment she had the chance, she scooped up her puppy and ran to catch up with the others.

'Come back!' the officer yelled after them, but

he didn't chase them far. Instead, he shrugged and went back to fighting the flames.

'Cool!' Lauren sighed, once she realised that the man had given up the chase. She and Buster stopped in the entrance to an office block, waiting for the others to join her. Finally, they all sat on the cold marble steps to catch their breath. 'Hey, thanks for rescuing me,' Lauren said.

Megan and Caitlin smiled. 'Don't thank us – thank Dylan and Daisy,' Caitlin said. 'They were the ones who led us to you.'

'How crazy was Russ,' Lauren sighed, 'jumping in the water like that?'

'Maybe he's a good swimmer.' Megan showed them her crossed fingers.

'Don't lose any sleep over him,' Lauren said. 'I mean – don't get me wrong – I don't want him to drown, but he did tie me up. And he did steal a diamond necklace.'

'What? How come?' Caitlin and Megan fired questions at Lauren.

So Lauren told them how Russ had snatched the precious necklace and stashed it in his pocket. 'Joey didn't trust him, and now I can see why.'

'Can you remember anything else?' Megan prompted her.

'The other one – Eddie – had hurt his leg, and Joey asked him if he could make it to Mickey's. That could be important, couldn't it?'

Megan nodded. 'If we knew where this Mickey lived.'

'But there must be a thousand Mickeys in Sleuth City, Caitlin sighed.

'Oh, and Russ told Joey on the phone that he'd meet him at Mickey's place!' Slowly Lauren fitted the puzzle together. 'So it definitely *is* important!'

Megan sighed. They were running out of time. From the steps of the office block she could see a hint of pink in the eastern sky. 'Anything else?' she asked Lauren hopefully.

'Yes. Joey and Eddie mentioned Dino. Dino was supposed to leave the upstairs window unlatched at the jewellery shop. There's no window at the back, so they had to use the front.'

'But Dino let them down – the window was locked so they had to smash it!' Caitlin picked up Lauren's excitement.

Megan nodded. 'You know what this means? Dino must work at Royale!'

Dylan wagged his tail.

'But he chickened out of being part of the

robbery; Lauren suggested.

'Yap!' Buster jumped up and raced down the steps on to the sidewalk.

'Which means he's in trouble with Joey and Eddie; Megan decided. 'Which is going to make him really scared when he realises they went ahead anyway – knowing he'll have to face them eventually.'

The girls stood up and dusted themselves down.

'So, we all know where we're going next?' Caitlin asked.

'Yip! Yap! Woof!' Daisy, Buster and Dylan chorused.

'Royale Jewellers, here we come!' Megan and Caitlin cried, running after the pups towards the highway as the sun rose over the river and the grey sky turned blue.

Chapter Seven

The crime scene on Fourth Street was still cordoned off when the girls and their pups arrived. A police officer stood guard at the jewellery shop door.

'So, how much did the raiders get away with?' a pushy reporter asked a smartly dressed woman standing inside the cordon. Half a dozen other journalists pushed and shoved to get in on the action.

The woman was obviously a manager at the store. 'I can't tell you exactly,' she replied cautiously. 'All I can say is that they knew what they were doing. They chose the most valuable designer pieces.'

'Are we talking gems worth thousands or millions?' the reporter asked.

The manager paused. 'Millions,' she confirmed.

There was a buzz among the journalists. This was a major heist, worthy of front page billing. 'How did they get through your security system?' one asked.

'We don't think they did.' The woman grew more nervous as the questions came thick and fast. 'It seems the thieves came in through the front door, posing as customers, just before we closed yesterday evening. Somehow they managed to slip into a storage area at the back of the shop. The police think that's where they hid while we set the alarms.'

'When you say "we", that would be you and who else?' the first reporter asked.

'It was myself and an assistant, Dino Whyte.'

Caitlin, Megan and Lauren had been taking in every detail, while the pups sleuthed and sniffed right up to the shop door. At the mention of Dino's name, the girls nodded eagerly.

'The question is – where's Dino now?' Lauren wondered.

'So, this raid is going to hit your business hard?' Another reporter asked.

The woman nodded. 'We're closed until further notice,' she replied.

As the journalists turned off their recorders, a kid of about twelve pushed through the crowd. 'Hey!' he yelled. 'Are you Haley Hartman?'

He'd shoved past Megan and now stood just in front of her. She took in his short cropped dark hair, his sticky-out ears and wide mouth, plus his blue T-shirt and jeans.

'Who wants to know?' the manager asked.

'I've got a message from Dino,' the kid called. 'He asked me to tell you he can't come in. He's sick!'

Caitlin and Lauren groaned.

Hayley Hartman came forward. 'Who are you?' she asked.

'Nobody – I'm just his cousin,' the boy muttered.

'OK. Tell Dino not to worry. We had a raid. The shop is closed anyway.'

'I'll tell him,' the kid promised, turning around and making off.

Straight away Daisy, Buster and Dylan stopped investigating the scene of the crime and began to track Dino's young cousin. They wove through the crowd of journalists and trotted after the boy, past the bank and the fashion shops, through the entrance to a shopping mall.

'Come on!' Caitlin said to Lauren and Megan. 'Let's follow the action!'

They had to move fast. The kid had long legs and was breaking into a run. He'd seen the pups following him and got a glimpse of the girls not far behind.

'This sucks!' Megan moaned as they turned into the busy maze of small shops and cafes.

'The pups won't lose him,' Caitlin reminded her.

Sure enough, Dylan, Daisy and Buster kept the boy in their sights. He tried to shake them off by darting into a clothes store, and out again through a side entrance. Then he disappeared into a music shop, taking the up escalator and getting stuck behind a bunch of teenagers.

'Now's our chance!' Lauren told Megan and Caitlin. They and the pups raced up the stairs and stood ready to cut the boy off at the

ROCK & POP ↑
↓ D. V. D'S

top of the escalator.

'Will you quit following me!' he said, angrily trying to barge past the girls.

But Dylan, Buster and Daisy had him surrounded.

'Where's Dino?' Megan asked, coming straight to the point.

The boy's eyebrows shot up in surprise. 'What's that to you?' he snapped.

'Listen – we know Dino's got himself into a tough spot,' Caitlin confided. 'He already knows about the robbery, doesn't he?'

This time, the boy's eyebrows shot up so high they nearly disappeared into his hairline. 'You'd have to ask Dino,' he shrugged.

'We will, if you tell us where he is', Lauren said.

The boy spread his hands, palms upwards. 'Why would I?'

'Because he's in trouble with Joey and Eddie,' Lauren told him. 'You're Dino's cousin – right?'

'Yeah. I'm Jay Whyte. We're like brothers, Dino and me.'

'Then you care about what happens to him.'

The pups let Jay step on to the down-escalator and the girls followed him. He headed out of the store into the busy mall. 'Of course I care!' he insisted with a sigh. 'You're telling me that Dino is mixed up in this jewellery shop heist?'

'He was meant to leave an upstairs window open so Joey and Eddie could escape.' Caitlin laid out the facts. 'And I'm guessing he was the one who helped them hide in the store room in the first place.'

'Oh, jeez!' Jay let out a long sigh. 'No wonder Dino wouldn't come in to work.'

'So now will you take us to him?' Lauren demanded. 'If we talk to him and persuade him to go to the police, they'll let him off lightly.' She didn't know for sure, but she reckoned it was worth a try.

'And Dino's supposed to trust *you*?' Jay shook his head. 'A bunch of strangers with three crazy, yapping dogs?'

As if on cue, Daisy, Buster and Dylan wagged their tails and yipped.

'They're not crazy…' Caitlin protested.

'I'm still not about to trust you,' Jay decided.

'If you won't let us see Dino, you must tell him to go to the cops,' Lauren insisted.

Jay frowned. 'It's not that simple,' he told them. 'You don't mess with Joey Morelli, believe me.'

'So your cousin's scared of him?' Megan asked.

'Everyone is scared of Joey! I never met the guy, and *I'm* scared of him!'

Lauren sighed and nodded, remembering her time in the getaway van. 'I understand that.'

'We all get it,' Megan agreed. 'Anyway, Jay, you can still do one thing for us.'

'Which is?' He started walking away, then changed his mind.

'Tell us if you know someone called Mickey.'

Lauren and Caitlin nodded. Good thinking, Megan!

But Jay shook his head. 'Mickey? No, it doesn't ring a bell.'

'Straight after the robbery, Joey and Eddie were heading for Mickey's place,' Lauren insisted.

'Mickey's place?' Jay thought hard. 'Oh, you mean "Mickey's Place"! Mickey isn't a person, it's a pool hall down by the riverside. On Lower Dock Street.'

'A pool hall!' Lauren grinned. 'Thanks, Jay – that's so cool!'

It was the girls' and pups' turn to break away.

'Don't get in too deep,' Jay warned. 'Remember what I said about not messing with Joey!'

But Megan, Lauren and Caitlin weren't listening. They had a new lead – and they weren't going to let it go cold.

CHAPTER EIGHT

'No kids allowed,' the guy on the door at Mickey's Place told Lauren, Caitlin and Megan. Then he frowned at Buster, Dylan and Daisy. 'And no dogs. This is a members-only club.'

'We were just looking,' Caitlin said, as casually as she could.

'There's nothing to see,' the bored doorman insisted. 'Just a whole lot of pool tables and a workout room at the back – a few weights, a running machine, that kind of thing.'

Megan nodded. 'I guess a lot of people want to join?'

'There's a waiting list,' he confirmed, yawning

as he spoke. 'But we're not busy right now.'

'So it's empty?' Caitlin followed up Megan's question and tried to peer past the front door into the dark interior.

'Why do you want to know?' the doorman asked. 'Are you looking for someone?'

'No, it's OK!' Lauren broke in. She was unhappy standing here in broad daylight, in case Joey and Eddie showed up. 'We're just hanging out. Come on, you two – let's go.'

'Better give those pups their morning walk.' The doorman yawned again.

'Let's go!' Lauren insisted, growing more uncomfortable than ever.

Mickey's Place was in a downmarket area close to the Sleuth City docks. Trucks and vans crawled along Lower Dock Street, delivering goods. There were no office workers or shoppers on the sidewalks – just builders and dockers in their hard hats and tough boots.

'OK, see you!' Caitlin told the doorman, allowing Lauren to drag Megan and her away from the entrance.

'What's wrong?' Megan hissed at Lauren as they took refuge in a poky coffee-shop doorway.

'We were attracting way too much attention,' Lauren sighed.

'Sorry,' Megan murmured. 'You're right, Caitlin – we need to be more careful.'

'Maybe we should take a look around the back of the pool hall.' Lauren decided on their next move. 'We'll follow the pups and this time we'll let them do the talking!'

There was a side street by the café which led to the docks. It opened out on to a stretch of river lined by tall cranes and yards stacked with containers. At the farthest edge of the container yards ran a narrow riverside footpath.

Looking tinier than ever under the cranes and multi-coloured containers, Buster, Daisy and Dylan set off. They were alert and eager, running along the footpath, followed by the girls.

'Whose scent are they following now?' Megan wondered.

They watched Dylan and Daisy hold back and let Buster take the lead. The little mongrel seemed sure of himself, ears pricked and tail wagging.

'Buster knows something that the others don't,' Caitlin decided.

The girls followed nervously as Buster turned from the path, crossed a wide concreted area and entered an alleyway. The alley opened on to a car park behind a low brick building.

'This is the back of Mickey's Place,' Caitlin realised. 'This car park must belong to the pool hall.'

'It's practically empty,' Megan muttered, counting only three cars and one flat-bed truck.

'But this is where Buster wanted us to come, for sure,' Lauren insisted, watching her pup race over to the solitary truck.

Buster jumped up at the vehicle, inviting Dylan to leap on to the back bumper and spring inside the truck. Daisy tried hard to follow, jumping up on her little legs and falling short.

'Buster is saying "Hide in the truck!"' Lauren decided. She wasn't keen to take his advice after her experience in the back of the thieves' van, but she trusted her pup, so went ahead.

She and Megan climbed into the open truck and ducked out of sight. Then Caitlin scooped up little Daisy and followed. Last of all, Buster leaped in after them.

'Heads down!' Lauren warned at the sound of a car engine.

The girls and the pups lay flat and made no sound.

Car brakes squealed as a car sped across the car park. Doors opened then slammed shut. Footsteps hurried towards the building.

'The back door's unlocked!' a man's voice said. 'Let's open the trunk!'

Lauren gasped. 'That sounds like Eddie. And I bet Joey's with him!'

'Sshh!' Caitlin warned.

They listened again, this time to the sound of scuffling and a muffled yell.

'I have to take a peek!' Lauren whispered, carefully raising her head.

'Don't let them see you!' Caitlin pleaded.

Holding her breath, Lauren peeped over the side of the truck.

She saw with a shock that the two thieves were dragging a third man out of the boot of their big, black car. The man struggled, but his hands were tied and he was helpless.

'They've got a prisoner,' she reported to the others. 'I don't recognise him... They're carrying him towards the building... Eddie's opening the door, they're hauling him inside!'

Bang! The back door swung shut.

As soon as Caitlin and Megan raised their heads, a boy on a bike raced into the car park.

'Jay!' Megan, Caitlin and Lauren chorused.

Dylan, Daisy and Buster leaped out of the truck and ran to meet him.

'What are you doing here?' Lauren asked.

'Following the car that drove off with Dino!' Jay was out of breath. He threw down his bike and ran towards the black limo.

'You mean, Joey and Eddie kidnapped your cousin?' Megan checked.

Jay nodded. 'After I left you I went straight over to Dino's apartment. I was waiting for the elevator on the ground floor when the door opened and Joey and his sidekick bundled Dino out. Dino gave me a look – totally scared. I was too shocked to say anything.'

'But you came to your senses and decided to follow the car on your bike?' Megan quizzed.

'I jumped a couple of red lights on the way,' Jay confessed. 'I thought I'd lost them, but the traffic held them up too, and here I am!'

'We just watched them carry Dino into the building,' Lauren explained. 'Don't worry – they didn't see us.'

'Is he OK?' Jay asked. 'He was alive and everything?'

Caitlin nodded. 'Tied up, but OK.'

'Did Joey look mad?'

Another nod from Caitlin confirmed Jay's fears.

'Dino didn't do as he was told. Now Joey wants to make an example of him.' Jay hung his head, his shoulders slumped. 'That's why they came for him.'

'So, we have to make a plan to get him out of there.' Lauren spoke firmly.

Jay looked up as if he couldn't believe the offer of help. 'Really?'

'Yes, really!' Megan told him. 'That's the reason we're here – to solve the crime and stop anybody from getting hurt!"

CHAPTER NINE

'How about this for a plan?' Megan said.

She, Lauren and Caitlin talked to Jay in the car park while the pups waited patiently by the back door of the pool hall.

'Step number one – we sneak Dylan, Daisy and Buster through that door and give them a while to scout around inside.'

'How long?' Caitlin asked. She didn't like the idea of sending the pups in by themselves.

'Not long,' Megan assured her.

'They can look after themselves,' Lauren added.

'Step two – Dylan, Buster and Daisy track

down Dino, then come back and take us straight to where he's being kept prisoner.'

'Can they do that?' Jay asked, staring down at what he thought were three cute, but ordinary, pups.

'You bet!' The girls nodded and smiled.

'Yip! Yip! Yip!' Buster, Daisy and Dylan chorused.

'Step three,' Megan continued. 'We creep in and follow them.'

'Daisy and I will stay by the door and keep guard,' Caitlin offered.

'And if anyone comes and asks what we're doing, I'll be ready with a big story about trying to round up our naughty pups,' Lauren decided.

Megan nodded. 'Jay, we'll follow Dylan. We'll double check that Joey and Eddie aren't around.'

'But what if they are?' Jay saw a flaw in Megan's plan.

'We wait,' she told him. 'Sooner or later their guard will be down, and that's when we move in and set Dino free.'

The others thought for a while then nodded. 'Let's do it!' Jay said, taking a deep breath.

Step one – Dylan, Daisy and Buster sneaked into the dimly-lit building. Shutters on the windows kept out the daylight. The girls and Jay glimpsed a room filled with gym equipment before they let the door swing closed.

Step two – they waited.

'I hate this bit!' Caitlin groaned.

The pups were gone for one minute, two minutes, then three.

'I can't stand it!' Caitlin's heart was thumping, her mouth felt dry.

At last Lauren heard paws scrabbling against the door. She opened it to let Buster, Daisy and Dylan through.

'Did you find Dino?' Megan asked Dylan.

Her little black Lab yapped and wagged his tail.

'Good boy!' Megan stroked him. 'OK, now show us where he is!'

Step three – the riskiest part.

'Sit!' Caitlin told Daisy. She stationed herself by the door, eyes peeled.

'Let's go!' Lauren said to Buster. They crept into the building, weaving between the cycling machine and the weights. Megan, Dylan and Jay were close behind.

'I'm glad it's still too early for many people to be around,' Lauren whispered.

But then Buster heard footsteps approaching down a corridor. He gave a warning whine. 'Quick, you go ahead!' Lauren whispered to the others.

A door swung open and an old man in a pink polo shirt, dark shorts and trainers walked in.

'Buster, come back!' Lauren made a big fuss as Buster scooted between the man's legs.

Meanwhile, Megan and Jay swiftly followed Dylan through a door marked "Shower Room".

'Oops, sorry!' they heard Lauren say in a loud, brash voice. 'I know we shouldn't be here, but...'

Inside the shower area there were rows of lockers and wooden benches. Beyond this there was a glass door leading to the showers themselves.

Through the glass, Megan and Jay saw two shadowy figures leaning over a third man crouching in a corner.

Jay's eyes widened and he lurched towards the door. Megan grabbed his arm. 'Wait, like we planned. Listen!'

'We're disappointed in you, Dino', Joey's muffled voice said. He sounded cold and mocking. 'We give you a little job to do and you mess up big time.'

'I'm sorry, Joey. I would've done it if I could. My manager, Hayley – she's real strict.

She checks all the windows and locks personally.

'You should've found a way', Eddie told him. 'Whatever it took'.

'Like I said, I'm sorry', Dino stuttered. He slumped in the corner and fell silent.

'You're a loser, Dino', Joey told him. 'But lucky for you, you're talking to a hungry guy who needs his breakfast'.

'Yeah, lucky you, Dino!' Eddie echoed.

'So, I'm going down the road to order two eggs over-easy and three rashers of crispy bacon', Joey went on. 'Eddie will be on duty outside the Shower Room door. No one comes in, no one goes out, while I'm eating. When I'm done, I come back down and decide what's going to happen to you, Dino'.

'Please, Joey – just let me go. I won't say anything to anyone!'

Hiding behind the lockers, Jay bit his lip. Megan kept a steady hand on his arm. 'Stay out of sight', she warned. 'Sshh, Dylan – not a sound!'

Joey obviously meant what he said about breakfast. Or maybe it was just to keep Dino hanging on in a fog of fear. Whatever the reason, he came through the frosted glass door with Eddie limping after him, leaving Dino tied up and slumped in the cubicle.

'OK?' Jay whispered as the two thieves left. Nerves were getting to him.

'No, wait. We have to work out how we'll get Dino past Eddie.'

'There are two of us against one of him,' Jay reminded her. 'Plus the puppy. Plus your two friends and two more pups outside. I reckon we can charge straight through.'

Megan gave a quick nod. 'Let's do it!'

Jay rushed into the cubicle. 'Dino, it's me – Jay!' he said rapidly. 'We'll get you out of here!'

His frightened cousin mumbled as Jay and Megan untied him. 'Nightmare... Joey had a knife... I thought I was a dead man!'

'You're OK, we won't let it happen,' Jay promised, helping Dino to stand. 'You see that door? Eddie's standing guard, but the plan is that we charge out – and *wham* – we knock Eddie flat and run!'

'Ready?' Megan asked. She checked that Dylan was by her side. 'Three, two, one – go!'

Together they barged at the Shower Room door. They heard Eddie shout and topple forward, then they shoved the door open.

'Follow me!' Jay told Dino.

Megan saw Eddie pull out a mobile phone. 'Grab it, Dylan!' she hissed.

So Dylan bit Eddie's hand and snatched the phone, dodging as Eddie tried to grab him. Eddie missed and Dylan sprinted off.

But Eddie was scrambling to his feet and chasing them across the gym. Dino stumbled against a rowing machine and tripped. The man in the pink shirt was staring open-mouthed at the commotion. Dylan and Buster snarled at the limping Eddie, who was yelling at the top of his voice.

'This way, quick!' Lauren held open the back door.

Dino picked himself up and made it outside with Jay.

'Go!' Caitlin told them. 'Grab the nearest cop. Tell them everything!'

'What about you three?' Jay wanted to know.

'We'll find you later,' Lauren assured him. 'Just go, will you?'

So, Dino and Jay set off across the car park towards the riverside footpath.

Back in the gym, Megan, Dylan and Buster tried to block Eddie's way.

'Charlie, go get the doorman!' Eddie yelled at the man in the polo shirt.

Then Joey burst through the inner door. He took in the chaos and his eyes turned colder than ever. 'Stay right where you are, Charlie,' he ordered. 'In fact, why not go down the street and have a coffee? Let me sort this out.'

Without a word the man called Charlie did exactly as he was told. He left the room and disappeared down the corridor.

For a few seconds, everyone froze.

'It's OK, Jay and Dino got away!' Lauren cried, dashing in from the car park with Caitlin and Daisy. She stopped short and gasped.

'Well hello again, everyone!' Joey mocked, motioning for Eddie to shut the door and lock it. 'This *is* cosy.'

Daisy, Buster and Dylan growled and crouched low, while Megan, Caitlin and Lauren all held their breaths.

'*Real* cosy,' Joey said, stretching his thin lips into a smile.

CHAPTER TEN

Lauren was the first to try and break out. She made a run for the door, but Eddie pushed her roughly away. She crashed against the wall.

Caitlin helped her back to her feet.

'Anyone else fancy a bid for freedom?' Joey sneered. Then his face turned deadly serious. 'You kids are a big nuisance. And you're way out of your depth, you know that?'

Trying not to show their fear, Caitlin and Lauren stood shoulder to shoulder with Megan.

'What next, Joey?' Eddie demanded. 'How do we stop these three spilling the beans to the cops?'

Joey's cold stare seemed to drill right through Megan, Lauren and Caitlin. 'Don't worry, no way will that happen,' he muttered. He was annoyed by a knock on the inner door. 'Not now, Charlie!' he snapped. 'Didn't I tell you to mind your own business?'

'It's not Charlie. It's me – Russ!' a voice said. 'Let me in.'

The girls gasped. 'I don't believe it!' Caitlin groaned, scared she was about to see a ghost.

Silently, still with his eye on the girls, Joey slid the catch and opened the door. 'Hey, Russ. What kept you?' he muttered.

Russ pushed his way in. He was dressed in a clean shirt and jeans. 'I went for a midnight swim in the river, that's what kept me…' Russ launched into explanations, then stopped as he noticed the girls and the pups. His jaw dropped as he recognised them.

Daisy, Dylan and Buster crept towards the newcomer, ears flat to their heads, growling from deep in their throats.

'Call them off!' Russ said. He wiped sweat from his forehead.

Caitlin, Megan and Lauren frowned, but did nothing.

'OK, I take it you want to get down to business?' Joey asked Russ. He seemed to think that Russ's fear of the pups was funny. 'Did you get rid of the van?'

Backing away from Dylan, Buster and Daisy, Russ nodded. 'Ask the kids – they saw me set light to it.'

Joey slid a sideways glance at the girls. 'OK, so we agreed on a ten per cent cut,' he reminded Russ. 'The jewels are at my place. I already had them valued at two and a half million. It would have been more, but we dropped the best piece on the way out of the building – a diamond necklace worth a cool seven hundred and fifty thousand.'

Caitlin and Megan gasped again, but Lauren's mind immediately went into action.

'You didn't see any sign of the missing piece when you cleared out the van, did you?' Joey checked with his accomplice.

Russ looked him in the eye and shook his head.

'Ten per cent of two and a half million gives you two hundred and fifty thousand,' Joey calculated. 'You get ten thousand now and I hand over the rest when I've sold the gems to an out of town contact.' He drew a wad of notes from his pocket and began to count.

Lauren braced herself and stepped forward. 'Ask him again about the diamond necklace,' she told Joey. 'Do you honestly think you can trust him?'

Suspicion flickered over Joey's features. He narrowed his eyes as the pups pushed Russ into a corner. When he spoke, his words were slow and deliberate. 'OK, Russ. I'm asking again – did you see the missing piece?'

'OK! OK!' Russ put his hands up. 'I did see it – yeah. The kid with the fair hair was hiding in the back of the van. She grabbed it after you and Eddie left.'

'And you snatched it from me!' Lauren insisted. 'You shoved it in your pocket.'

'To give back to you, Joey!' Russ gabbled. 'Honest, I swear I put it in my pocket to bring here!'

'So?' Joey asked.

'Where is it?'

'Like I said, I had to take an unexpected swim,' Russ told him. He kicked out at the pups, who nimbly dodged his boot. 'It's a long story, but I had to get away from these three. So I jumped in the water. When I climbed back on to dry land and searched my pockets, the necklace was gone!'

Joey drew a sharp breath. 'You're telling me that jewels worth three quarters of a million are lying in the mud on the river bed?'

'On my life!' Russ swore.

'*Grrrr!*' The pups moved in again. Daisy pounced and sank her teeth into Russ's left ankle, while Dylan grabbed the right one.

'Hey, that hurts!' Russ yelled.

It was Buster who jumped and pushed Russ back against the wall. And it was Buster's sharp teeth that ripped the pocket of Russ's jeans, splitting the stitching and showing Joey the sparkling necklace nestled inside.

'You dirty cheat!' Joey moved in to grab the necklace. He swung a punch at Russ and hit him in the stomach.

'Nice work!' Caitlin grinned at Lauren.

'Go, Buster! Go, Daisy! Go, Dylan!' Lauren cried.

'This is just what we needed!' Megan grinned.

Eddie had joined the fight and the three men were brawling and sprawling, tearing and pulling, socking each other with giant punches.

'Let's hope they knock each other out!' Caitlin muttered, calling Daisy and heading towards the exit.

The three villains were breathing heavily, still fighting hard when four cops broke down the door and burst into the room.

'Police!' the sergeant yelled. 'Everybody, stay right where you are!'

CHAPTER ELEVEN

'The robbers were caught red-handed!' Megan and Caitlin let Lauren give the news to Hayley Hartman, the manager at Royale Jewellers. 'Joey Morelli had dropped a diamond necklace on the floor. Buster grabbed it and sat with it dangling from his mouth when the cops ran in!'

'He looked dead proud!' Caitlin grinned.

'So cute!' Megan added.

'And we'll get all the jewels back?' Hayley stared at the odd assortment of kids and puppies gathered by the shop door.

'All of them,' Jay promised. 'And if we didn't

already have enough evidence, Dino has promised to be a witness in court, telling how Joey and Eddie used force to make him cooperate with them.'

'So *he* let them into the store room?' Hayley checked.

Jay nodded. 'But only because Joey held a knife at his throat.'

'So, where is he now?'

'With the cops, giving them all the details.'

Lauren, Caitlin and Megan listened, hoping that Dino wouldn't be charged.

'I hope he gets his old job back,' said Lauren.

'We won't be around to see,' Megan reminded her.

'At least we know Eddie and Joey will spend a long time in jail.' Caitlin gave a satisfied sigh.

'Thanks, as usual, to Dylan, Buster and Daisy!' Lauren grinned.

'High five, Dylan!' Megan crouched and held up her hand to the little Lab.

Dylan raised a paw.

'High five, Daisy! High five, Buster!' Caitlin and Lauren smiled.

The two pups sat on their haunches and put up their paws. High five!

'We've got to go now, Jay,' Lauren said.

'Me and Dino – we didn't thank you properly yet,' Jay protested.

'That's OK. You're welcome.' Megan blushed, then pointed at Dylan who was already trotting off down the street. 'Like Caitlin said, we have to go!'

'Ready?' Lauren asked.

The pups had headed into a small park off

Fourth Street. Now they sat in a row, looking up at the girls.

Caitlin and Megan nodded. 'Chasing criminals is hard work,' Megan admitted.

'So, let's take off the pups' medallions,' Lauren said. 'One, two, three – go!'

Together, they removed the gold medallions. A wind blew through the green trees, a bright white light appeared.

'Whoo-ooo!' Caitlin cried, as she rose into the air with Daisy.

'Cool!' Lauren grinned, as she and Buster soared upwards.

'Home, here we come!' Megan called. She and Dylan flew up above the trees, off into the clouds.

Read more adventures
in the **Mystery Pups** series

DOGNAPPED!

A missing pooch, a mystery text message, and a
tearful little rich girl – what on earth is going on in Sleuth City?
The Mystery Pups are about to find out!

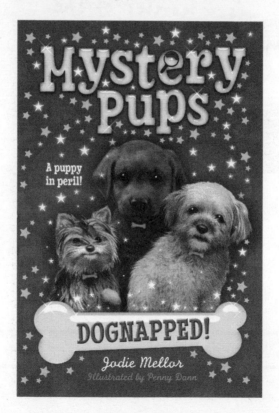

978-1-84738-224-5 £4.99

FRAMED!

The Mystery Pups are back in Sleuth City.
A valuable painting has been stolen and
the wrong person is being blamed. That is
until the Mystery Pups get on the case!

978-1-84738-225-2 £4.99

MISSING!

The feline star of a major movie is missing!
If the Mystery Pups don't find the famous
kitty in time, there's going to be trouble...

978-1-84738-226-9 £4.99